REUNION

Bachelors in a Bind: Book 1

Enola Wilder

Six Sirens Press

Reunion

Copyright © 2024 by Enola Wilder

All rights reserved.

Book Cover by Najla Qamber, Qamber Designs

Edited by Anjali Didier

First edition 2024

For Anjali Didier. I couldn't have done this without you, my friend.

"You should probably wake up now. He's been waiting for you for a very long time."

Contents

1

O n a hot night in August, Faolán stood under the shadow of
the Washington Arch, unmoving, like a boulder in a river, as
a current of New Yorkers flowed past him and spilled out into the
moonlight.

He stepped to the side as a pack of sharp-suited men in fedoras
pushed past, trailing smoke and laughing at the tail end of a dirty joke.
He pulled a postcard from his jacket pocket, and the simple act of it
sent his heart racing.

Across the front, "Greetings From Massachusetts" in bold red let-
ters, obscured a sketch of Boston Harbor. On the back were words he
was almost too embarrassed to read—desperate, clumsy descriptions
of longing and remorse, addressed to a friend he hadn't seen in five
years.

Thankfully he hadn't sent that one, or the other one still folded
in his pocket. He wasn't sure why he was still holding onto these
aborted attempts. The one he had finally sent had been stripped of all
sentiment, whittled down to a simple request.

***

Luca,

Meet me Saturday night at 9:30 at the fountain in Washington Square. I'm turning 20.
Abyssinia,
Faolán

***

He regretted extending the invitation the moment the postcard disappeared into the depths of the mailbox. He even contemplated trekking up to East Harlem in the hopes of somehow stealing his mistake back. But what was done, was done, and standing Luca up after five years apart would forever torment his conscience. He had to see it through.

There were countless reasons why Luca might not show up. Maybe he hadn't gotten the postcard in time, or maybe he'd be busy that night at his father's tailor shop, or on a date somewhere. But no matter the outcome, he owed it to Luca to be where he promised to be.

Young couples had taken over the wooden benches that lined the park paths and the stone steps circling the fountain, sitting shoulder to shoulder and holding hands, and, when the mood overtook them, leaning in for a kiss. Faolán found an empty spot on the steps by the water's edge, away from the light of the park lamps, and settled down to wait. He unzipped his jacket to cool off, and set his leather satchel by his side. His watch read just past nine, he still had a while.

Even if Luca did show up, there was a chance they might not recognize each other. When he'd left for Boston five years ago, Faolán was still scrawny for his age, and wiry. "Like a sad, pale spider dragging books into his web instead of flies," Luca had called him long ago when he'd borrowed too many library books and struggled to carry them all home. At the time, Faolán had been mortified by the comparison, but now he remembered the words fondly.

From time to time, the pull of a hand, or the wake as someone waded past, sent ripples across the surface of the water and shattered the night sky into swirls of light. Faolán did the best he could at straightening up his shifting reflection, buttoning his collar and sweeping his sandy brown hair beneath his flat cap, the hold of his pomade having long faded. He leaned in as the ripples pulled him apart and pieced him back together again.

He pulled out another postcard and traced his finger across a red and white lighthouse set against the Nantucket skyline. He made sure no one was looking before he turned it over.

***

Luca,

I should have told you I was crazy about you before I left. I've thought about you every day. Meet me at the fountain. You know the one.

Yours,

Faolán

***

He pushed it below the water's surface and watched his confession blur and fade. He made his birthday wish early.

Stop thinking about him that way.

His longing for Luca tended to flare up like summer allergies, the symptoms relentless in their severity, lasting weeks before they worked through his body and he could breathe again. Being apart had made the feelings easier to swallow back down, but he didn't know why he couldn't shake this bout, why his thoughts of Luca inevitably drifted to what his mouth might taste like, or what might happen if they met again. This fever had raged since he returned and he just wanted it to fucking break.

Another reflection joined his in the water, their features blending together, almost undecipherable as to where one ended and the other began until the water stilled and Luca remained.

"Is that you, Fae?"

Faolán looked up at the sound of his name, Luca's voice unmistakable, though lower than he remembered. It had been a long time since anyone had called him by that nickname, and the sound of it, the fondness wrapped around the word unsteadied him and sent his heart racing.

In the years since he'd last seen him, Luca had somehow grown from a messy-haired, bruise-knuckled teen into a matinée idol with his high cheekbones and dark eyes, his black hair perfectly parted on the side and swept back. For a moment Faolán feared the Luca he'd known was gone, replaced by a dashing bachelor in a chalk-striped, wide-legged suit, who probably sought out more distinguished company, until Luca flashed him a familiar grin that said, "Let's get into some trouble, you and me."

"Yeah, it's me. You really came?"

"You invited me," Luca said.

Luca took a step back from the fountain's edge and held out his hand. Before Faolán could reach out, Luca had him by the wrist and hauled him to his feet. He almost stumbled as he stood, barely grabbing his satchel on his way up, but Luca caught him by the shoulders and pulled him into a tight embrace.

Faolán froze, pressed against Luca's strong chest, his arms limp at his sides, gripping the strap of his bag so it wouldn't slip from his fingers and into the fountain. Luca's cologne smelled of wood and spice, and Faolán stopped himself from sinking into him, closing his eyes, resting his head on his shoulder. Breathing him in. It would be so easy to.

"Isn't your birthday tomorrow?" Luca asked against Faolán's ear. "I know it's been a while, but I think I'd remember-"

"Oh, well yeah... I just figured you wouldn't wanna stay out late on a Sunday."

Luca laughed and let him go.

"I'm just givin' you a hard time. God damn it, look at you. You got some real muscles on you. You're almost as tall as me now?"

Luca was being generous. It was true he'd gotten taller and stronger, he'd hit a growth spurt at fifteen and broadened out but he was still lean compared to Luca and about two inches shorter. Faolán stared down at his battered brogues, Luca's black and white Oxfords looked like they'd been spit-shined.

"Yeah, I guess I grew up some," Faolán said. "You did too. Never seen you in a suit before."

"You like it? Like the gangsters wear. Tailored the pants myself."

"You got real good. Back in the day you were always finding excuses to get outta the shop."

"Times have changed, my friend. Anyway, it's your birthday, I figured you wanna get some drinks, maybe go dancing? I know just the place. You still trust me, right?"

"Yeah, of course."

"Then let's go." Luca wrapped his arm around Faolán's shoulder and set off down the path.

Greenwich Village bustled around them, filled with the energy of a Saturday night. Luca weaved through the crowds, nodding at the ladies outside jazz clubs and vaudeville theaters. Faolán picked up his pace to keep up with Luca's long stride. They stopped on Sixth Ave, beneath the El, as the trains rumbled and sparked high above. Faolán buried his hands in his pockets and tipped his head back, waking up as the city buzzed around him. Luca did a quick look in all directions.

"You sure you know where you're going?" Faolán asked.

"Course I do." Luca pointed west. "We're headed to the right place for the wrong people. It's just another block. Maybe two."

"I got no idea what that means."

"Café Society. I know you'll love it. It's bohemian, full of artists and leftists. Right up your alley. You're still an artist, right?"

"That doesn't go away, you know."

Luca commandeered Faolán's arm and they set off again.

The streets narrowed and grew quieter as they weaved through the West Side. Brownstones and street lamps replaced the wide avenues and bright storefronts.

If Faolán had any money at all, he wouldn't mind living in a place like this, with the park close by and all the art and music that flourished in this neighborhood. Luca slowed his pace as they reached West 4th, a line of patrons stretched around the block. The crowd was an eclectic mix, black and white, all young and stylish. They mingled together in small groups, gentlemen in dark suits and fedoras on the arms of young ladies in evening dresses and spring coats, some with bright flowers in their hair.

Faolán took watch at the back of the line as Luca circled the block on reconnaissance. The place had to be good to draw a crowd like this. By the look of the crowd, it seemed like a fair amount of the ritzy uptown contingent had migrated south to see what the fuss was all about.

Luca returned wearing a grin that meant they might have a chance.

"So, it looks like this show gets out in forty-five. If they don't hit capacity for the next one, we should be able to get a spot in the back. Billie's singing tonight. You know who she is, right? Lady Day? We gotta try if that's still okay with you."

"Yeah, I know who she is. If you like the place, I'll wait for it."

"You're gonna love it, I promise."

The conversation faded after the consensus, and Faolán found it easier to study the crowd than hold Luca's gaze. He searched for something to say as the silence stretched out between them. It had been so easy years ago. Words had flowed between them without effort and for hours on end. But now a heaviness had settled between his collarbones and his words were unable to push past.

So far, the night had gone nothing like he'd imagined. Luca hadn't greeted him with a blow to the face, he didn't seem to be mad at him for his disappearing act and the years of silence that followed. But he still wasn't sure.

"How've you been?" Faolán asked.

"Good. Living above the shop now. Got a deal on the place 'cause we've been tenants for so long and my dad managed to keep up on the rent when a lotta folks couldn't."

"He probably did that so you'd finally get to work on time. Your pop's no fool."

Luca seemed to brighten at the jab. Faolán tried not to laugh.

"You should've put your address on that postcard. I would've come seen you." Luca said. "I couldn't get that far with just 'Brooklyn'."

"Yeah, I know…"

"It's no matter, you're here now, right? You're staying? Tell me what you've been up to."

"I got a city job through the WPA if you can believe it. It's with the poster division, but I'm the greenest guy so I only do touch-up work."

"But you're making a living doing art. That's what you always wanted. I'm really happy for you. Honest."

Another wave of silence pushed through Faolán, bringing sadness with it this time, at how much he had missed him. There were so many things he wanted to ask but didn't know how. Stupid little things like when Luca started wearing cologne or what he'd had for breakfast that morning, to the bigger questions, ones that might break his own heart.

"I think I'm underdressed." Faolán said instead, frowning at his wrinkled button down shirt, his jacket half-zipped to hide the ink stains he'd gotten on it earlier that day. His gray slacks were cuffed neatly, though still a little too long. He'd managed to get most of the scuff marks off his brogues after twenty minutes of polishing that morning, but even that didn't help much. Standing there, in the middle of a sharply-dressed crowd, wearing the one flat cap among a sea of stylish fedoras, he'd missed the mark by a mile.

"What are you talking about? You look great."

"More like square."

"Here, I'll loan you this. It's real silk."

Whatever resolve Faolán had set in place cracked around the edges as Luca tugged his tie loose and stepped closer. Faolán kept his hands at his sides and a careful smile on his face, as Luca slipped the tie around his collar and worked on making the perfect center knot.

"You okay? You look a little tense."

Faolán nodded, trying his best not to be brought down by a glancing touch or Luca's hand at his throat. He hit his limit when Luca unzipped his jacket and adjusted his suspenders to get the clips even. He pushed Luca's hands away.

"Not exactly a match with brown suspenders, but there you are. Faolán Donovan, man about town."

"I'm not so sure…"

"You say that a lot."

Faolán ran his fingers down the navy silk, then realized he'd grown too quiet and launched into a rambling monologue about his day to make up for another round of awkward silence. He'd spent half the day working at home on his first solo assignment so he'd have something to show on Monday, then caught a Rex Bell cowboy double feature in Times Square to pass the time. After that got out, he wandered through Chelsea to see how it had changed in his absence and found a new deli he'd never seen before.

And when his story ended, and Luca started up with tales of his day working at the tailor shop and all of the strange customers who passed through, Faolán's heart slowed, fairly certain that Luca hadn't noticed that his ears had gone red back when the tie was looped around his collar, or that he'd lost the ability to put a sentence together until Luca stopped touching him and stepped away.

At a quarter to midnight, the line moved.

As they closed in on One Sheridan Square, Faolán weaved his way from the crowd to get a better look at their destination. From the outside, the venue seemed modest, sandwiched between a beauty salon and a food market, Café Society in white script across a faded maroon awning. A wiry, young man stood guard at the door, decked out in a battered top hat and a greatcoat coming apart at the seams.

"Citizens, we are at our limit for the night," the doorman yelled. "You are more than welcome to come back tomorrow, albeit maybe earlier next time. Shows are at eight, ten, last one right now. Six nights a week. Better luck to you all. Tomorrow."

Luca cursed and pulled out his Luckies.

"I'm sorry. I made you stand around for nothing. I just wanted you to see the inside at least. They've got these giant murals all over the walls. You would've liked it. We passed a few bars on the way, let me at least buy you a drink."

Faolán took Luca by the arm and guided him out of the path of the dissipating crowd. The doorman sat on a wooden stool by the entrance and pulled hard on his cigarette, his top hat set on the ground beside him.

"Give me a minute," Faolán said, as a plan formed in his head, "Let me try."

"No, really it's alright-"

"One minute." Faolán held up his hands until Luca stood down. "Maybe five. Wait here."

"You want me to talk to him? I've got a way with people."

"Yeah, I know you do." With the way Luca looked now, he could probably flash a smile and sweet talk his way through the door, but he wanted to give Luca this one. "Leave it to me."

Luca leaned back against the wall, beside the row of posters showcasing the night's roster: 'Comedian Extraordinaire: Jack Gilford.' 'Albert Ammons, Meade Lux Lewis, and Pete Johnson: The Best of the Boogie Woogie Pianists!' 'Billie Holiday Sings the Blues.' Most of the names didn't mean much to Faolán, but Billie Holiday he knew well. Luca frowned at the list like each name held a place in his heart.

Tasked with a mission, Faolán's determination slid into place. Getting into the club didn't matter to him, he'd be happy to find the closest bar and celebrate his birthday beside his oldest friend, but Luca had his heart set on showing him the place, so he had to get them through the door.

The doorman watched as he approached. Faolán followed the path of the man's gaze, first to him, then to where Luca stood, before locking back on him once more. The doorman exhaled a perfect ring of smoke. Faolán took off his cap.

"I know you're on your break right now... and I'm sure people come up to you all the time wanting to get in after the doors close." Faolán paused, leaving room for a response, but the man stayed silent. "See, my friend over there, the guy looking sad by the posters. He's a huge fan of Albert Johnson."

"Pete," the doorman said. "Pete Johnson."

"Yeah... honestly, I don't really know them, but he does. He could tell you everyone they've ever played with, and everything about them." Faolán had no idea if this was true, but once he found the thread of a tale, he could spin it in any direction. "I know we can come back tomorrow, but if there's a little room in the back, just enough for two, maybe we could stand there? In the back?"

Faolán waited through another uncomfortable bout of silence before he began to back away.

"I'm sorry, I shouldn't have bothered you. We'll try again tomorrow like you said. You have a good night, sir."

The doorman stood and put his top hat back on. He flicked his cigarette butt into the street, set his hands on Faolán's shoulders, and leaned in close like he was about to let him in on a secret. His mouth brushed against Faolán's ear. His breath smelled of smoke and liquor.

"Look buddy, if you want to impress your fella by getting him in tonight, I'm not gonna argue with that. You've got yourself a real looker over there."

Faolán opened his mouth, taken aback by the boldness of the statement, yet flattered by the assumption that somehow Luca was his. When no words came out, he nodded.

The doorman waved for Luca to come over and bowed low as he approached. Faolán prayed he'd keep their exchange quiet.

"Welcome to Café Society. You fellas enjoy your evening."

Luca shook the doorman's hand.

"Wow, what did you say to him?"

"I don't remember."

"Did you tell him it was your birthday?"

"Just get inside before he changes his mind."

As the door closed behind them, the rumble of the club drowned out the sounds of the city. Faolán stood off to the side of the coat check girl after losing the battle for buying his own ticket, the words the doorman had whispered to him still going round in his head.

A mural of a pale, waif-like woman stretched out across the ceiling, her waist cinched in a corset of red roses and a gramophone horn where her head should be. Her long, gloved arm pointed toward the stairs. Faolán stepped aside and let Luca lead the way.

The air grew thick and hot as they descended, and the stairs emptied into a small basement space, with standing room all the way to the back. Faolán imagined the club would be sprawling, but it held maybe two hundred people at most. Surrealist murals covered the walls and Faolán squinted in the dark to make sense of the curious forms. He'd have to take a closer look at them later if he had the chance, see if he recognized the artists. A row of tables lined the front of the stage and circled the dance floor.

Faolán lingered on the stair to take it all in. He set his hand on Luca's shoulder to keep him there awhile longer.

"What do you think?" Luca shouted above the din. "You like it?"

"Yeah, It's really-"

"Aces, right?"

"Definitely."

A lone comedian had the room in stitches. Jack Gilford it had to be, as he was the only one listed on the poster outside. He strode back and forth across the stage, making fun of the latest movies and pulling faces like he was made of elastic, mimicking Clark Gable and Charlie

Chaplin and even Shirley Temple without missing a beat. By the end of the act, Faolán knew the endings to six movies he hadn't seen yet and his sides ached from laughing.

As the stage lights dimmed, and the comedian finished his encore, Luca turned.

"The guy upstairs said Billie's going on first, so I'm gonna try to get us closer. I'll signal you when I have something. If you spot a girl you like, maybe I can introduce you later."

"It's alright in the back. I gotta good view from-"

Luca disappeared into the crowd. Faolán didn't bother to finish his sentence.

The room held its share of lookers for sure, some ladies had the air of film stars about them, poised and elegant, with their long dresses and swept-up hair. Though if he had to pick a girl from this crowd, he probably wouldn't go for a glamorous one. Maybe someone simple, like him, who liked looking at buildings and figuring out the shapes of things. Someone who laughed easily and didn't mind a guy who was prone to melancholy and day dreaming. But at that moment, the last thing on his mind was looking for a match—his heart already yearned for the one who'd walked away.

He looked up when he heard his name. Luca stood by a small table in front of the stage, waving for him to come over. There were two others with him, but he couldn't make out more than bright dresses and the back of a stylish hat. Faolán waved in return and stepped into the crowd. He excused his way through the sea of bodies, spinning apologies, careful not to bump into anyone holding drinks. When he was close enough, Luca latched onto his arm and pulled him ashore.

"Reiza, Seraphine, this is Faolán Donovan. He's been twenty for about fifteen minutes, just moved back to New York, and has never been to a jazz club. Wait, is that true? I don't know what he got up to in Boston... Faolán, these are the Pascal sisters. It's Reiza's last night in New York, so like us, Billie Holiday was in order."

Reiza and Seraphine were as opposite to each other as he was to Luca. Seraphine stood almost a head taller than her sister, decked out and glamorous in pale gold with skin like Josephine Baker, her thick, black waves arranged in an elaborate up-do. Reiza seemed to be the more reserved of the two, in a simple pale blue dress and a hat to match. She adjusted her glasses after she shook Faolán's hand.

"I really hope you don't mind us sitting with you," Faolán said. "We were the last to get in. I was fine standing back on the stairs, but Luca's always been very serious about his music."

"Seraphine made me promise good conversation and a spin on the dance floor in exchange for their company," Luca said, "I think she let us off easy."

"You boys are more than welcome to join us," Seraphine said.

Reiza made space and let Faolán and Luca sit between them.

Faolán settled down next to Reiza, determined not to be awkward. He couldn't deny the disappointment that their reunion now included the company of others, and that Luca seemed more alive and in his element now than he'd been all night. But Reiza had a kind smile, and seemed like she might be easy to talk to. He moved his chair closer.

"So, what kind of name is Faolán?" Reiza asked. "I've never heard it before, but I like the sound of it."

"It's old and Irish. Means wolf."

He waited for Luca to point out that his name actually meant "little wolf," like he'd always done when they were younger. But Luca was already lost in a light-hearted debate with Seraphine over who sang a better ballad, Sarah Vaughan or Ella Fitzgerald. The two lit up and laughed as they traded favorite lyrics and songs and compared the shows they had seen.

"I'm not sure what mine means," Reiza said. "But it's a family name, so I think I was lucky to get it."

"I had an uncle Faolán, but I never met him. They said he was wild-spirited and ran off with a pale woman who lived under the hills."

"Are you like your uncle? Wild-spirited?"

"No... Can't say that I am."

Reiza smiled like she didn't believe him.

"You're leaving tomorrow?" Faolán asked. "Had enough of the city?"

"No, the opposite really. Just going back home to pack up some things, put my affairs in order, then I'll be running back here as fast as I can."

"So, you must be the wild-spirited one. Your sister's not going back with you?"

Reiza patted his hand gently.

"So, tell me, what do you do, Mr. Wolf?"

Faolán hauled his bag onto the table and pulled out his sketchbook. He wasn't sure why she changed the subject so quickly, but it wasn't his place to ask. After some searching, he found the page he was looking for, filled up with singing barbers drawn in every style and combination, combs in their pockets and razors in their hands.

"You know that singing contest they got every summer in Central Park? For barbershop quartets? I get to make the poster for it this year. I guess that's what I do for a living now. Make art for the city."

"WPA? I've got two cousins up in Harlem who got teaching jobs through them. You've got a good eye."

Reiza flipped slowly through his sketchbook, pausing on each page to study his work. She stopped at one of his more detailed drawings from atop his rooming house. He'd climbed up to the roof early one Saturday and spent the morning translating the skyline. Manhattan

Bridge on his right, Brooklyn Bridge on his left, filling up the sky with clouds as a summer storm rolled in. He resisted the urge to explain each image and let his work speak for itself. He didn't share this side of himself with strangers often.

She stopped once more at a page filled up with rough sketches he'd made of naked models from a life drawing session he'd been to. Young women frozen in dynamic poses, most no more than half finished.

"Ah... Sorry, I forgot those were in there. They're not anything. I just take art classes when I can..."

Faolán reached over to turn the page. Reiza covered his hand with her own and leaned in close.

"You do know we're not really sisters, don't you?"

Faolán shook his head, not sure what to say.

"Phine just likes to say that when she isn't sure about the company."

"I'm not sure what you mean..."

"You might not be wild-spirited, but you do seem kind. And the way you and your friend watch each other when you think the other isn't looking. That makes me think you might be the right company. If you catch my meaning."

Faolán stared down at Reiza's small hand, her short nails painted pink, the silver band on her ring finger engraved with roses. It would be easy to deny it, or feign offense, or tell her that Luca and he were only friends. Because as far as he knew, that was the truth.

"I'm sorry, I didn't mean anything by it," Reiza said. She pulled her hand away and closed the sketchbook.

Faolán leaned closer, lightheaded by the possibility, "He's really been watching me?"

Luca bumped Faolán's shoulder, startling him back into the moment.

"Hey, Seraphine wants to know how we met each other, she thinks we look like an odd couple."

"I didn't say that at all," Seraphine said. "But I'm learning that Luca quite likes to stretch the truth to make a girl laugh."

"You wanna tell it, or should I?" Luca asked. "Now Fae knows how to tell a good story. You get him going and he'll make you believe there's mermaids swimming in the East River and men living on the moon."

"Is that so?" Reiza asked.

"Not mermaids, selkie, and yeah, I did have him thinking there were men on the Moon. But, no, you go ahead."

Faolán sat back in his chair, turning over Reiza's words, not sure if there had been truth in them. He pushed them down and focused on Luca, determined not to be caught stammering if the conversation turned back to him.

"It's really not that exciting," Luca said. "His ma worked for my family for almost ten years. Mrs. Donovan brought him along at the start 'cause he was too small to be left at home. Of course, my ma, saint that she is, thought it'd be a good idea if I kept an eye on him. Keep him out of trouble."

"You know that whole "keep an eye on him" part was to make sure you wouldn't put me out with the empty milk bottles. I was small and pale, so they might have mistaken me for one."

"Don't be fooled, he's just trying to get some sympathy from the crowd. I tried my best to keep him out of trouble until his ma and new dad packed him off to Boston, but he definitely didn't make it easy for me."

"How long were you gone?" Reiza asked.

"Five years. We only went 'cause they had jobs lined up there. '33 was terrible."

"Well, I think it's sweet that you're still best friends," Seraphine said.

Faolán managed to smile at Seraphine's words, though each one felt like a blow. Sitting at Luca's side, he couldn't tell how Luca took the comment and he didn't want to search his face for the answer. Luca pulled his Luckies from his pocket and tapped the edge of the pack against the table.

"All that being said," Luca broke the silence first. "He's probably one of the best guys I know."

"Probably?" Faolán said. He tucked his sketchbook back into his bag, uncomfortable with all of the attention.

"Well, I'm starting to ramble so I guess I should bring this in for a landing. Happy Birthday, Fae. I'm glad you made it back home."

Faolán looked down as everyone cheered and Seraphine let loose an impressive whistle. Luca lit up a cigarette and slid the pack to Faolán and although he hated the taste and never picked up the habit, he pulled one from the crumpled pack and set it between his lips. He leaned in towards the flame Luca offered and inhaled slow and deep.

"After this, we should go someplace quieter, you know... to talk," Luca said. He leaned close so Faolán could hear him over the noise.

Faolán held the smoke in his lungs, hanging onto every word, distracted by Luca's closeness, until the back of his throat burned and he burst out coughing. Luca slapped him on the back. Faolán covered his mouth and turned his head away.

"You alright?"

Faolán nodded once his breathing began to settle, eyes watering, the attention of the table turned on him now. Luca's hand stayed steady against his back.

"You don't smoke, do you?"

Faolán shook his head as Luca tugged the cigarette from his fingers and stamped it out in an ashtray. He tucked it behind his ear.

"You didn't have to take it. You know you can be on the up and up with me, right?"

"Yeah. I'm sorry." Faolán said between breaths, holding still in the hope that the connection might remain.

"It's no matter…"

In the long pause, as conversations around them came to a close, and everyone waited for Lady Day, Luca's hand still lingered between his shoulder blades for a few moments longer before he pulled away.

In the center of the stage, a single point of light broke the darkness, and a warm spotlight illuminated the space. Billie Holiday stepped from the shadows, white gardenias in her black hair, the hem of her long gown brushed the floor as she walked barefoot across the stage and into the light. She stared out across the shadowed crowd, the sky-colored silk of her dress pale against her skin, catching the light. As the piano played, she reached out her hand, drew the microphone close to her heart, and started to sing.

Swayed by the melancholy tide of her song, Faolán leaned back in his chair as a lethargy spread through his limbs, and the long hours of the day caught up with him. The room softened around the edges.

And after a while, perhaps the ground shifted beneath him or the earth tipped on its axis and Faolán leaned in its wake and his shoulder came to rest against Luca's. He watched Billie through half-closed eyes, her body swaying as she sang of love and loss, her eyes closed against the light. The sadness and yearning in her voice felt uniquely like his own, but he didn't want to feel those things, sitting so close to someone he shouldn't be sweet on.

His hope hadn't been born from nothing. As they grew older, Luca started running the streets with guys that were never mentioned or introduced to him, guys who came from Luca's neighborhood, with names that didn't sound like his. He didn't truly understand what it meant until he broke down and followed when he shouldn't have, and caught Luca backed up against a brick wall, making out with a guy in a quiet alleyway. A guy who had beaten Faolán up once, in another quiet alleyway.

Luca stared up at the stage. Riveted on Billie, he closed his eyes, lost in the song.

Faolán found his bearings slowly and sat back in his chair to put a respectable distance between them. He searched for the courage to be bold and wild-spirited, to show Luca that he could be more than just a friend if he wanted.

And as Billie's song pulled at his heart, Faolán held his breath and set his hand on Luca's thigh. Billie's voice faded into the background, replaced by his racing heartbeat, and the moment stretched on until Luca tensed beneath his touch. Faolán looked down, his hand seemed unnaturally pale against Luca's dark trousers, maybe a trick of the light, but he didn't know what to do now.

The stage lights faded to black as Billie ended her song, and the crowd burst into applause. In the darkness, Luca locked his hand tight around Faolán's wrist. He leaned in close.

"Whatever nonsense you're thinking right now. Just fucking stop."

2

Faolán pushed through the crowd, his head down, bodies around him reduced to a blur of color and sound. He stopped short, again and again, making near misses of waiters and patrons, refusing to look up and navigate. He didn't have a destination, only a direction, away from what he'd done. He'd stood up too fast when Luca let go of his wrist, jerked his hand away like he'd been burned, leaving everything behind as he fled. By the time the house lights came up, Faolán found himself sitting at the bar on the far side of the club.

A mural of animal patrons stretched across the wall behind the bar. Faolán sat across from a solemn-looking wolf, dressed up in its Sunday best, black spectacles balanced on the end of its snout. He wasn't sure if the wolf was meant to be his reflection or a window to another world full of creatures instead of men. In that world, he would be no more than a painting of a solemn young man. A man who lived in his head too much, whose best clothes weren't quite good enough, and who had made a grave mistake that night. Faolán broke eye contact with the beast. His wrist ached where Luca had grabbed him.

He ordered water when the bartender came, still bristling from the embarrassment of getting everything so wrong. He stayed very still and kept his back to the crowd until Billie finished her last encore and the house lights came back up once more.

It would be easy to get up and leave, to walk out the door and into the night. Luca probably wouldn't want to see him after what he'd done. He weighed those thoughts, as the water soothed his throat and the glass cooled his fingers before he landed on doing what he knew to be right. Reiza and Seraphine had been nothing but kind to him, he owed them at least an apology and a proper farewell. He didn't know what he'd say to Luca, he'd figure it out when he got there.

Luca wasn't at the table when he returned. His bag had been set on his chair and his jacket folded neatly beneath.

"Are you alright?" Reiza asked. "Luca went looking for you. I packed up your things, I wasn't sure..."

"We were planning to meet up with some friends after this at Club Hot-Cha," Seraphine said. "You're welcome to come with."

"I'm sorry I left so suddenly. I wasn't feeling well. It's been a long day..."

Faolán pulled on his jacket, not sure what to do next, wishing the night hadn't gotten so far away from him. If he could go back in time and do it all over again, he would have sat on the other side of Reiza and kept his hands to himself.

"When he gets back, will you tell him I'm sorry? I know he might've had more planned, but I should head on home. I really enjoyed meeting you both." Faolán shook their hands once more and tried not to read into the concerned looks they both gave him. "Tell Luca I said he should stay. It'd be a shame if he left early on my account. Have a safe trip tomorrow, Reiza."

"Are you sure you're alright, Faolán?" Reiza asked, and the worry in her eyes broke his heart a little.

"Yeah, don't you worry," Faolán lied. "I promise."

Faolán paused outside the club to settle his nerves and try to put everything behind him. His ears rang in the stillness, the streets quiet now that the crowds had gone. A lone taxi idled at the end of the block, waiting for its last ride of the night. The doorman stood at his post, leaning back against the wall, watching him. Faolán braced for a remark, but none came.

He wasn't too far from where the night had started, he could head back to the park and settle on a bench until the sun rose. East would take him to the Sixth Avenue El and from there back home to Brooklyn. That seemed like the soundest choice, the most sensible one. But as he was neither of those things at that moment, he went west and turned down Seventh Ave. to get away from it all and get lost on the long streets.

He buried his hands in his pockets and kept his head down as he left the bustle of the clubs behind. He tried to fill his head with things other than what he'd done, but the moment played over and over again and he couldn't get it to stop. He forced it down, distracting himself with street names and store signs, and how much he hated love songs, as Seventh Ave. became Varick and he kept on walking. Reiza's dress had been the color of the sky, and he wished he'd asked her how she'd met Seraphine, and when they had fallen in love.

A closed-up Chrysler Plymouth lot took up part of the block ahead, its painted signs lit up under bright lights, promoting the best of new and used cars and payments as low as four dollars a week. Faolán stopped in front of a sleek '36 Imperial, its pale, blue body polished so brightly he could see his reflection in the shine. Not the most expensive car, but far more than he'd ever afford. He'd have to return another time and sit with his sketchbook when his nerves stopped buzzing.

He walked on, down empty and quiet streets, wrapped up in his thoughts until a low rumble pulled him back to the present. Halfway down the block, a large black car stood in his path, pulled up on the sidewalk and blocking the mouth of an alley. At that distance, the details were hard to make out, but its wide silver grill and headlights looked familiar, and he could easily tell it was far nicer than any of the Chryslers he'd passed. As he approached, the smooth curve of the pontoon fenders, pristine whitewall tires, and the Flying Lady hood ornament told him what he needed to know. He'd never seen a Cadillac Phaeton up close, only in magazines and in the movies. Parked before him, it seemed too perfect to be real.

Two young men leaned against the front of the car. They passed a silver flask between each other and laughed at something Faolán couldn't quite hear. Uptown boys by the look of them, dressed up for a night out, suit jackets gone, shirtsleeves rolled up to their elbows. By the state of them, the way they swayed a bit when they leaned close and shushed each other when he got closer, it looked like they'd been at it for most of the night.

With the Cadillac blocking his path, his only option forward was to walk into the street and go around, even though he didn't want to take the long way. Not for a car that shouldn't have been stopped there, and not for guys who were probably looking for trouble. Faolán slowed a few feet from where they stood, then thought the better of it and picked up his pace.

"That's right, just keep on walking."

Faolán ignored the jab and stayed quiet. Although neither of them had the roughed up look of brawlers, it was still two against one, and Faolán had never taken to fighting.

As he stepped out onto Varick, the passenger door of the Cadillac swung open in his path. Faolán caught the door before it slammed into his chest and the force of the impact sent him staggering back. The two men burst out laughing.

The man who climbed out of the car was broad-shouldered and thick, and unlike the other two, still in his suit jacket. Whatever he'd used to slick back his dark hair had given way and thick strands fell forward into his eyes. His nose looked like it had been broken at least twice. He slammed the door closed and stared down at Faolán.

"What the hell are you doing, running into my car like that. If you scratched it, I'm going to fucking kill you."

"Running into you?" Faolán said, his palms still stinging. "I know you saw me coming."

"That so, huh? I'm a liar now?"

A taxi cab rumbled past, its lights on, headed uptown, and Faolán imagined himself half-asleep in the back seat, drifting away from everything that happened that night, and everything in front of him now.

"No... I didn't- I didn't say that. Look it's late," Faolán said, "I've had a fucking terrible night, so how about we all just go-"

"How bout we all go? How bout we all go where? What, you wanna come with us?"

Faolán glanced down at the car door, not a single mark on the paint. He stifled the urge to say anything that would kick off a fight, and focused instead on the giant blocking his path, more than a head taller and at least twice as wide. The two men who had been leaning against the Cadillac left their perch and moved in behind him.

"Tommy come on, just let him go. We got girls waiting."

"Don't be a fucking wet blanket, Albie. They can wait. I got this guy here calling me a liar."

Faolán stayed quiet, if the past five years had taught him anything, it was to know when speaking up would get you knocked down. Albie, the one who'd wavered was the slightest of the three, blond hair slicked back, his hands didn't look like they'd thrown a punch in a while. Faolán had two names now, which was good, he liked to know who he was up against. Tommy was the leader of the pack though, and if he barked loud enough, his dogs would fall into line.

Tommy stepped closer, bringing with him the stench of alcohol and too much cologne. He dropped a heavy hand onto Faolán's shoulder. Faolán dug in and stood his ground. If he backed up, they'd all come for him, if he ran, it would be worse.

"Alright, alright, I'm just joking with you," Tommy said. "You can run along home..."

Faolán bristled at the pause, bracing for the demand that always followed. He knew this game all too well, mastered the slippery rules of cruelty with his stepfather when he was in Boston. He closed his hand into a fist and braced for what was coming next.

"...after we shake on it. You know, so there's no hard feelings."

Tommy offered Faolán a meaty hand, the gesture nothing more than a dare. Gold rings wrapped around his fingers and a gold watch hung loosely around his wrist.

The two men at his back grew quiet.

Faolán extended his hand and Tommy reached past and grabbed him by the wrist and pulled him close.

"And once you apologize."

"I didn't do anything," Faolán said quietly, his words slow and deliberate as Tommy's grip tightened, grinding the bones in his wrist.

"You know, I was hoping you'd say that."

Faolán drove his fist forward, aiming for Tommy's gut and his hand collided with a wall of muscle and fat. The force of the impact rippled back through his arm.

Tommy laughed off the punch and slapped Faolán hard across the face and the shock of it, the indignity of being struck like that lit him up from the inside. Light shone around Tommy like a halo as everything slowed and Tommy's laugh stretched out into one long sound. Faolán brought his arm up to block another blow, adrenaline dampening the pain. Tools and books clattered onto the ground as his satchel slipped from his shoulder. He swung again, too slow and too wide and then he was on his back on the street, not quite sure how he'd gotten there.

"Slap him a few times and he goes down faster than a girl," Tommy said. "You gonna start bawling now?"

Tommy kicked off the next round of laughter then stopped and glared at his guys until they joined in.

Rough hands hauled Faolán off the street and shoved him into the alley. He struggled to get his feet under him, blood in his mouth, his left ear ringing from the blow. If Tommy had punched him, he'd be out cold right now—the bastard had dukes like fucking bricks. Faolán backed up slowly—his way out of the alley blocked by the Cadillac and Tommy's men so his only choice was into the dark.

Tommy came at him again, grinning like a lunatic and Faolán knew the bastard was looking to break him. Faolán pulled himself into order: fists up, chin down, body angled, weight low. He stood his ground deep in the alley, a shuttered-up repair shop at his back, Tommy between him and the way out. Albie and the other one ripped through his bag and dumped what was left inside onto the ground.

Tommy closed the gap, momentum and spite driving him forward. Faolán knew he had to put distance between them, if Tommy got his hands on him, it was over. But standing alone in the middle of this goddamn alley, two hours into his birthday, and at the end of one of the worst nights of his life, Faolán stood his ground and swung like he was channeling Joe Louis. His right hook slammed into Tommy's jaw, scraping across teeth and snapping Tommy's head back. Faolán pulled back and got his guard up fast. The roar that came out of Tommy, made Albie and the other one stop and pay attention.

Tommy shook off the hit like getting punched in the head was a common occurrence. He dragged the back of his hand across his mouth, blood staining his teeth and knuckles red.

Digging in a second time would get him beat down fast so Faolán kept moving. The blood on Tommy's mouth brought a grin to his own, but he'd wounded Tommy's pride far more than his face. Albie and the other one moved closer to watch.

"You like that, Tommy? C'mon, you want more?"

Tommy roared and lumbered forward. Faolán knew he would pay for every one of his words with broken bones and blood, but the rage on Tommy's bloody face might just be worth it. Faolán scanned the alley behind him for anything he could use to even the odds.

Out of reach and mixed up with the debris scattered across the ground, there was something narrow and metal. He had no idea what it was, but if he could get a hold of it, he might be able to swing it hard and slow Tommy down.

Tommy swung wide and clumsy and Faolán reeled back and dodged the first punch, but the second came short and quick, and caught him in the stomach, knocking the wind out of him. Faolán doubled over and dropped to his knees.

The taste of blood filled his mouth as he dry-heaved and the night flickered in and out of focus. His heartbeat thrummed in his head, drowning out everything except the ragged sound of his breath not coming fast enough. He caught only half of the words Albie and Tommy traded, something about what they were going to do to him when he stopped moving.

Faolán pressed his hands against the ground, knuckles bruised and raw, pulled one knee forward, then the other, and forced his eyes open, trying to make each breath longer than the one before. Tommy crouched down beside him.

"You're going the wrong way, punk."

Faolán dragged himself deeper into the alley, towards the metal rod on the ground, the tip jagged and sharp, just out of reach.

Another shove sent him toppling onto his side, slamming his shoulder against the ground. Instinct brought his arms up to block the next blow, but Tommy knocked them aside and locked his hand around Faolán's throat. Faolán gripped Tommy's wrist, dug his fingers into skin, going for blood.

"You could've just said you're sorry and been on your way." Tommy pulled Faolán's face close to his own and tightened his grip. "You see what being a tough guy gets you?"

As the night around him darkened and blurred, a single thought pushed its way up and hovered before him: There was no way this bastard would be the one to put him down.

"Tom-" Faolán gasped.

"You got something to say to me now?"

"Yeah, I do." He would have said if he had enough air to form words. But instead, Faolán let go of Tommy's thick wrist and drove the heel of his hand into Tommy's nose, and broke it for the third time.

Tommy roared and covered his face and Faolán dropped back against the ground, finally able to breathe again. Tommy's blood splattered hot across his cheek. He braced for the next blow.

"Looks like I'm missing all the fun. Can anyone join?"

Luca's voice echoed from the mouth of the alley. From where Faolán lay gasping, the distance seemed like miles, but the sound of it broke through his haze and woke him up.

Luca entered the alley, drawing all eyes onto him. Albie and the other one closed ranks and blocked Luca's path. Tommy stood up, the front of his white shirt streaked with blood. He lumbered towards the new threat and left Faolán in the dark.

Faolán didn't waste the distraction, he struggled to get up again, but with the world spinning he only made it to his knees. He closed his hand around the broken tire iron. Once he could get upright, he could swing it, and if he got close enough, he could hurt someone. He gripped the metal until his hand stopped shaking.

"It takes all of you to take this guy down?" Luca said, "You need some help?"

"We got this under control," Albie said. "This is none of your business."

"No, I was talking to the guy on the ground."

Luca threw the first punch, striking Albie before he had a chance to get his hands up. Luca launched himself at the other one as Albie staggered back and hit the ground.

By the time Faolán got to his feet, Tommy was deep in the fray, his arm around Luca's neck, pulling him off his men. Luca threw his weight back, drove his elbow into Tommy's ribs, and slipped from his hold. He spun around to strike, and met Tommy's fist head-on. Tommy pressed forward, followed up with a hard right, and Luca's knees buckled beneath him and he went down.

Albie got up slowly, swaying as he blocked Faolán's path. He had his fists up this time, ready to fight.

Faolán tightened his grip on the tire iron, his eyes locked on Luca, who had his back against the ground, blocking Tommy's punches and slowing down. His only thought now was to get to him.

"Get the hell out of my way," Faolán said, his voice so quiet only he could hear the words. "Or I will fucking go through you."

3

Faolán opened his eyes, still reeling and disoriented, trapped somewhere in a flickering darkness. He struggled, held from behind, his arms pinned to his sides as blinding lights streamed past, then cast him back into shadows. Fragments of the night caught up with him and took shape. Luca had gone down in the alley. Tommy had caught him with a sucker punch and Luca had gone down.

From the backseat of a car, the city blurred by too fast for him to get his bearings. Faolán thrashed against the hold, his body slow, limbs heavy, the taste of blood still in his mouth. He let out a string of curses and a hand clamped tight over his mouth and pulled his head back.

"If you keep throwing punches, he's gonna kick us out of his taxi." Luca's whisper against his ear slowed him down and stopped his struggling. "You're alright, Fae. But you gotta keep it down."

"Everything okay back there?"

The question came from the front of the car, an old man at the wheel watched them through the rear view mirror. "You said there wasn't gonna be any trouble."

Luca loosened his grip and Faolán slumped back against him, the need to fight finally draining from his body. He untangled himself from Luca's arms and moved to the far side of the cab, putting as much space between them as the narrow seat would allow. His reflection blurred in and out of focus in the glass as the city flowed past, slower now, quieter now that he wasn't raging in the middle of it. A bruise darkened the corner of his mouth and the right side of his face was scraped up and bloody where Tommy's ring had cut him. It burned him, being marked by that bastard, that he'd have to carry the reminders on his skin until they faded.

"Yeah, we're fine now," Luca said. "No more trouble, sir. I promise."

The cabbie turned back to the road.

"You gotta tell the guy where we're going. You made me promise I'd take you home, but I still don't know where you're living now."

Faolán sat forward. He ran through his address slowly, down to the room number of his Brooklyn Heights rooming house. When he got it all out, he rearranged himself carefully until his back was against the door. The cool glass behind his head did little to ease the throbbing, but it calmed him to be upright, braced against something solid. Breathing deep ached, but the pain wasn't sharp and nothing seemed to be broken. He opened his hands wide then drew them back into tight fists. He hadn't gotten in enough blows to damage them too much, but his shoulder ached something awful and would for a while. He closed his eyes and tried to reconcile the jump between Luca on the ground, and Albie charging him, to being halfway to Brooklyn.

"You still with me?" Luca asked.

Blood stained the front of Luca's shirt and carved a sluggish path from a gash above his eyebrow. Luca wiped his forehead and frowned at the blood left behind on his fingers.

"Pop's gonna kill me, showing up at the shop like this…"

"How the hell did we get here?" Faolán asked. "That bastard hit you and you were on the ground and when Albie knocked me down, I didn't think I was getting up again."

Luca touched his nose gingerly and wiped away more blood.

"Leave it to you to learn all their goddamn names... That repair shop in the alley was closed, not empty. Not really an alley I guess. We must've made enough of a ruckus out there that a few guys came out carrying baseball bats. Everyone made tracks."

"So, it was just luck?" The weight of what the words meant settled heavily in Faolán's chest. "He was gonna kill me. For nothing. I could've got you killed too."

"What happened back there? Why were they on you?"

"Does it fucking matter?"

"Course not... Just glad I found you when I did."

Faolán kept his back against the door, turned away from the East River and the skyline as they crossed the Brooklyn Bridge, blocking out the view of the city that could make him feel like all was right in the world, because it wasn't.

Luca leaned back and grew still and his breath came deep and steady. Blood trailed from the cut above his eye and disappeared into his dark hair. Faolán dug through his pockets and found some change and the last of the folded-up postcards, but nothing to help.

He remembered his tie, Luca's tie, and tugged it from around his collar. He reached across the gap and pressed it into Luca's hand.

"Use this for your head. Hold it against it."

Before Faolán could pull away, Luca squeezed his hand and held on for what felt like too long before he let go.

Faolán retrieved his bag, tucked down by Luca's shoes. The shoulder strap had been ripped from one side, and the metal buckle that held it closed was bent and useless. His father had brought it with him from Ireland, and carried it for years before his mother passed it down to him, and each broken piece he found made him want to put his fist through the window. He took stock of what remained, everything inside battered and broken in some way. The cover had been ripped from his sketchbook, and a chunk of pages torn from his copy of *Brave New World*, but he was far past that point in the story.

He pulled the bag onto his lap and pushed down all the things he wanted to say, shoved them down to the bottom with the rest of the torn-up and ruined things. He didn't know how to say he was sorry, or even where to begin, so he didn't.

The weight of Luca's arm around his shoulder grounded Faolán as he startled out of a dark dream, once again slumped against Luca's side. He had been running through shadows, chased by something he couldn't see. Tearing open doors that led to nowhere, banging against doors that wouldn't open. Luca's voice behind them all. The cab slowed and stopped, back on his street, finally home. Faolán dug through his pockets for cash he didn't have. Luca reached across him and opened the door.

"Don't worry about it," Luca said, "I got it."

"I'll pay you back."

"No you won't, it's your birthday."

Faolán gathered up his belongings and stepped out onto the curb, and his knee gave out when he put his full weight on it. He steadied himself against the cab and tried again. He didn't remember hurting it, but he'd ended up on the ground so many times it was all kind of a blur. His knee held the second time, still aching, but he could manage. He lingered on the curb unsure if Luca was coming with or going home, then limped off, not wanting to seem like he was waiting around like a chump.

"Where the hell are you going?"

Faolán pointed down the block towards the end of a long stretch of row houses.

"Stay there," Luca said. "Don't go anywhere."

"I'm fine." Faolán stopped in the middle of the sidewalk, his bag tight under his arm, fully aware of how ridiculous the statement was. "Go on home. I can take care of myself."

"I know you can, but I'm not gonna let you." Luca caught up and slipped his arm around Faolán's waist. "Just shut up and lean on me."

Faolán relented and did as he was told. They walked in silence, Faolán leading the way down the narrow alley behind his building, the path he always took when it got too late to take the front entrance. He warned Luca to stay quiet before they entered and that the woman who ran the place lived on the first floor and didn't tolerate noise after 9 o'clock.

Luca reached into Faolán's jacket pocket to retrieve the keys.

"How'd you know they were there?"

"It's where you always kept them."

Together they crept up the stairs and past the bathroom that he shared with the three other tenants on his floor. He stopped at 304, the last door on the left and waited for Luca to open it.

Finally inside, he dropped his bag by the door and switched on the light, revealing the humble collection of things that made up his home: a small wooden table covered with dishes and art supplies and a sink in the corner that he'd paid extra for, a Murphy bed and a dresser, and an old loveseat by the window. He kept his prized Silvertone radio atop a bookshelf crammed tight with stories set in faraway worlds.

Luca wandered through the space with his hands buried in his pockets, looking at everything without touching.

Faolán ducked under the clothesline that bisected his room, careful not to displace his undershirts and clothes for tomorrow. He wrestled open the windows to let out the stale air and switched on the lamp on his dresser, bathing the room in soft light.

If he had known he was going to have company that night he would've put the place in some kind of order, make it seem like he didn't live in the aftermath of a tornado. He didn't want Luca thinking everything about him was chaos.

He paused by the window, good for now with the barrier of laundry and the space he'd set between them. Maybe during the fight, Luca's memory of his clumsy pass had been knocked out of him. Maybe the omission so far had been out of kindness.

"Let me get a better look at you," Luca said. "See what the damage is."

Luca stood at the sink, washing the blood from his hands and face. He studied his reflection in the mirror and poked at the cut above his eye, it went deep, but the blood had slowed. He rinsed out his tie until the water faded from red to clear.

Faolán cleaned up the best he could after Luca finished, then distracted himself by getting to work. The edges of his first-aid kit had long gone rusty, but the box still contained his suture kit and the rest of the essentials. He cleaned off his table, stacking used dishes and art supplies onto the shelves above and laid his findings out before him.

"I just got this today." Luca hung the dripping tie over the clothesline. "It looks like it's been through a war."

"You should let me stitch you up. It'll keep opening."

"Let me see your hands." Luca said, and Faolán held them out, palms facing the floor, his knuckles reddened and scraped up, the right worse off than the left.

"They're good enough to hold a needle steady."

"I'll be the judge of that. Do as I do."

Faolán mirrored Luca's movements, opening and closing his hands, wiggling his fingers until Luca nodded and seemed satisfied.

Focusing on the task of putting Luca back together made it easier to pretend that this night had been like any other, only unluckier than most. They'd run through this ritual over the years, taping up each other's cuts and scrapes so their parents wouldn't find out they'd been brawling, though usually with him in the chair and Luca the one piecing him back together.

"You don't need many." Faolán spot-checked the wound, making sure it was clean. "No more than two or three."

"If you say so."

"Don't flinch now."

"I'm not gonna fucking flinch."

He pressed iodine-soaked gauze to the cut above Luca's eye, staining the wound brown with the pungent antiseptic. Luca flinched, then stilled. Faolán tried not to smile.

"How did you find me?" Faolán asked.

"When I got back to the table, Reiza told me you'd left. She said I should go after you, that you were upset."

Faolán wasn't surprised that Reiza had seen right through him. His excuse had been so thin it verged on transparent.

"I was hoping she'd ask you to stay. I didn't want you to call it a night 'cause of me. Hold still."

Luca gripped the underside of the chair. His dark eyes slipped closed and a calmness settled over him as if he had drifted off. Pushing down the thought of kissing him came easier after everything that happened that night. Faolán stayed on task and made the first stitch at the center of the wound, guiding the needle tip through each side, careful not to go too deep. He made a neat double knot and moved onto the second.

"You're pretty good at this. Barely felt that one." Luca reached up towards the stitches. Faolán caught him by the wrist.

"Don't do that."

Luca lowered his hand.

"I asked the doorman if he saw where you went and he said he'd tell me only if I was gonna apologize to you."

"I swear I never said a word to him, I just stood on the curb for a while, then walked off."

"I told him if anything happened to you, I was gonna come back and drop him."

"You really said that?"

"Yeah, I wasn't fooling around. I only found you 'cause I went the direction he told me to, and kept walking till I ran into that Cadillac. I knew if I lost you tonight, I might never see you again."

Faolán grew quiet and focused on keeping his stitches straight and the line clean. After about five days, if Luca didn't poke at his handiwork too much, the scar would be thin and fade with time. He tied off the final stitch, cleaned the wound one last time, and covered it with a bandage.

"I guess you're as good as you're gonna get," Faolán said.

"Then it's your turn in the chair."

Faolán reluctantly traded places.

"It's not as bad as it looks. My head still kinda hurts... I cut up the inside of my mouth, but really, I'm okay." Not wanting Luca to worry, Faolán left out that his shoulder still ached where he'd landed on it, and he couldn't put his full weight on his knee yet. Pulling up the front of the shirt would reveal a patchwork of dark bruises across his ribs, so he kept quiet about that as well.

"Why don't you hold still like you told me to, and let me patch you up. Alright?"

Faolán set his hands on his knees and held still, thankful the hard back of the chair stopped him from pulling away.

"You did pretty good back there." Luca took Faolán's hand and examined his knuckles. "Are these teeth marks?"

"I don't know. I might've got a lucky one in."

"Give yourself some credit. You broke his damn nose. I saw that much."

Luca cleaned Faolán's hands methodically, liberal with the antiseptic and rough with the scrubbing as the words between them faded. Without the buzz of the city around them, the silence became the loudest thing in the room. Faolán bit his lip as the iodine soaked into his cuts and burned.

He stared at the floor, unable to hold eye contact as Luca took him gently by the chin and turned his face towards the light. Luca traced the line of his cheekbone, the caress both gentle and aching as Luca's fingers brushed across the scrapes and bruises the night had left on his body. He paused at the corner of Faolán's mouth, where the bruise marked his skin.

"I can't do anything for these." Luca said, breaking the silence, and any trace of the connection that had passed between them. He packed up the first-aid kit and put everything back where it belonged.

"I should go. It's a long way back to Harlem."

"It's late though... You don't have to."

Luca pulled on his coat, opened the door.

"You gonna be okay?" Luca asked.

There was no way to answer the question. Faolán wasn't even sure what Luca was asking him, only that it sounded final. The chair scraped against the floor as he stood, the sound far too loud for the late hour. Once on his feet, he froze, unable to figure out the right combination of words that would stop Luca from leaving.

Luca paused in the doorway, his back an impenetrable, unreadable wall. He stepped into the hall and closed the door behind him.

Dried blood speckled the toes of Faolán's shoes. He wasn't sure who it belonged to, it might have been his own. He would probably find more when he stripped down and climbed into bed. In the stillness, all the places where he hurt fought for his attention. Faolán stopped at the door and rested his forehead against the wood. The space seemed smaller without Luca in it.

"Fuck..."

He touched the bruise at the corner of his mouth, gently as Luca had done. The memory of it spinning back and starting again.

If he left now he might be able to catch up with Luca, have one more chance to show him that he was more than just the ghost of the friend he once knew. If there was even a chance to be friends again and nothing more, he would be okay with that. He would grab onto it and hold tight because just being in the room with Luca made it feel like home.

Faolán left the door open behind him, limped down the stairs and out the back door as quietly as he could. There was a pay phone at the end of the block, Luca would have made it at least that far by then, if he hadn't already picked up a passing cab. A few neighborhood bars would still be open, easy places to slip into. He didn't know how he'd find Luca in any of those, but he would try.

He rounded the corner and stopped. Half-way up the stoop in front of his building, Luca sat, lighting a cigarette, his attention fixed at a point somewhere across the street. Faolán sat down beside him.

"You're still here."

"Yeah. After I finish this, I'm gonna hunt down a cab."

The cigarette tip glowed orange-red as Luca inhaled. Faolán figured he had maybe six minutes and the only words that filled his head didn't make any sense. They probably weren't the right ones, but they were the only ones he had and silence was no longer an option.

"About a month ago. I went walking along the river. Really early, before the sun came up, to find a quiet place to sit by the water. Sketch the skyline while the world was still. And I waited for a while, until the sun rose up from behind me and the sky blushed and grew pale and blue, and then I saw her..."

Faolán paused. This would usually be the moment when Luca would chime in, ask him a question or throw him a look that said, "Oh, here you go again." But Luca stayed quiet, and stared ahead like he wasn't there, and Faolán feared that once again he was messing it all up.

"She came right up from under the water. About as close to me as the bottom of these stairs. Just floated there, black hair spread out all around her on the surface, her seal skin draped over her arm. These East river selkie, they're not like the hearty ones my father used to see off the coast of Howth or Greystones. She was pale and hollow-cheeked, and her eyes were black, like the depths of the river where she and her sisters swam. But even though she was quite frightening and I might have scooted back a little, so she wouldn't get any ideas about reaching up and pulling me under, there was a certain kindness in those dark eyes, a certain loneliness. And so we talked."

Luca lowered his head. In his worn out and disheveled state he looked more like Faolán remembered from long ago, the quiet Luca that sat beside him at the end of a fight, most of which had been started because Luca had stood up for him.

"I don't wanna hear one of your stupid stories, Fae. What are you trying to say to me?"

"She asked me about you. Knew you by name. Why aren't you with that dark-eyed one? You used to stick to him like a shadow. The one who could never see us. You're half-formed without your Luca. I told her that I'd gone away and though I never found any magic where I ended up, I did find monsters. I missed him every day we were apart. And when I was finally able to find my way back, I hoped he might still have a fondness for me. And maybe he would forgive me for fading away."

Luca stood, his movements sluggish as if the long night had gotten to him as well. He flicked his cigarette butt into the street, his face hovering between sadness and anger. Faolán knew that particular pain well. He'd lived with it for so long that it had become a part of him, burrowed into his bones.

"I wasn't planning on coming tonight," Luca said. "I tore up your damn postcard when I got it. I swore I wasn't gonna come, and then it was today, and then tonight, and then I was putting on my best suit, so worried I was gonna be late. That you'd have already left."

"Luca... I didn't-"

"Fuck you. I'm not finished. Five years. Not a word. Nothing. I know you didn't have a choice. I know you had to go with your family, that there was work up there. But you'd already backed away from me long before you left, and once you were gone, you were gone. It was like you died. And I always thought that it was my fault."

"No, it wasn't. None of it."

Faolán looked down, too self-conscious and too aware of Luca staring through him. The last thing he wanted was for Luca to have felt guilty, not for the silence that he had inflicted. He forced himself to his feet, afraid that Luca would leave again.

"I don't wanna tell you all the things that happened there," Faolán said. "Why I never wrote you. I wanted to. I really did. But those years, I was just trying to survive."

"Is that why you didn't wanna see me? When I came to Boston?"

Faolán froze, as each of Luca's words became a long needle through his heart, pinning him in place. Whatever came after drifted past without meaning, as he battered against Luca's question. There was no way this could be true, he would have responded. He would have come.

"No, you were never in Boston." Faolán backed away, trying to get away from what Luca had told him. He sat down on the stairs and covered his face with his hands.

"My family had business there and I went too, hoping I could see you. It was maybe a year after you moved there? I sent you a letter asking. I called your home when you didn't show. I was so scared that if I went to find a pay phone, you'd show up and think I hadn't come. The man who answered told me never to call you again."

The night grew quiet as Faolán tumbled back through the years, trying to remember when this all might have happened, and pinpoint the day when his stepfather chose to keep Luca from him. He lost track of everything around him, mourning the countless what-ifs that spiraled out in all directions. His head throbbed as he willed the tears not to come. He didn't want Luca to see him like that, but he couldn't form the words to tell him, too afraid of the sound he'd make if he tried.

"You really didn't know?" Luca asked.

Faolán flinched as Luca's fingers brushed against his, still covering his face, trying to keep everything from spilling out. He lowered his hands, dug his fingers into his knees to try to pull himself from the past. When he opened his eyes, Luca knelt before him. The night seemed darker somehow, and more gray than he'd noticed before.

Luca covered Faolán's hands with his own.

"He hated me," Faolán said. "All those years he just looked at me, knowing he'd kept you away... I'm surprised he never broke, just to rub it in. He must've been so pleased with that secret. I swear to you, if I had known, I would have come."

"I know."

"I would've waited all day for you..."

"Fae, I believe-"

"And I'm so sorry about tonight, I shouldn't have touched you like that. I don't know what I was thinking."

He found it far easier to stare at Luca's roughed-up hands now that he was so close. His regret was sincere, but his thoughts had been clear when he touched Luca's thigh. They'd been needful and had never gone away.

"Yeah, I'm sorry about that." Luca said.

"Why? It was my fault."

"No, it really wasn't."

Luca's hair slipped forward into his eyes as he lowered his head. Faolán watched Luca quietly, oscillating between wishing he could know Luca's mind and wanting to stay in the dark. He stopped himself from reaching out, sweeping Luca's hair back, feeling its softness as he tucked it behind his ear.

When Luca looked up, he seemed more certain. He pulled Faolán to his feet.

"We shouldn't talk out here."

Although the street was quiet, Luca was right, some discussions should be held where no one would hear. Faolán started down the stairs, slower now, still not quite all in his body. Luca took him by the wrist and pulled him back.

"I'm not going around the back again. We'll be quiet, like the Shadow, I promise."

Luca held out his hand and Faolán gave him his key, too tired to argue that they shouldn't be going that way. Luca played the part of the Shadow seriously, opening the front door without a sound and closing it just as quietly. They crept through the darkened foyer where guests waited during the day. Luca slipped the key back into Faolán's pocket, and took him by the hand until they made it back to the safety of his room.

Faolán offered Luca his chair and sat on the table, regretting the move immediately as his body ached with the effort. The last thing he wanted was Luca looking down at him, not when he already ached with regret.

"I'm sorry I was so hard on you," Luca said. "You caught me off-guard at the club. I didn't want you doing anything you were gonna regret the minute the lights came back on."

"I didn't mean to imply that you were... I didn't mean anything by it."

"Oh, come on. You know I've been with guys. You caught me in that alley years back, so I know you know."

"I didn't think you saw me."

"Of course I did"

"You know I hated that bastard, right?" Faolán said. "He always dug into me when you weren't around."

"Yeah, we didn't last outside that alley. By then you'd already cut me off. A whole month you didn't talk to me. Then you went to Boston and that's that. When you never came to meet me, I figured you must hate me or something. So no, I wasn't gonna let you show up out of the blue, make a pass at me, then never speak to me again."

Luca, I never hated you-"

"It's all so far in the past, Faolán. Let's just leave it back there. You don't have to be sorry about anything. Nothing really happened tonight anyway-"

"No, listen. Please? I didn't hate you," Faolán said, too loud and too fast, afraid more than anything that whatever door he might have cracked open would be shut and locked. "I was mad at you."

"For what?"

"I don't know... We were best friends and you never told me. I only found out 'cause I saw you with fucking Frankie Vitale. Took me a while to figure out I was mad 'cause you picked him over me."

"So what, you just stopped talking to me?"

"I didn't know what else to do. I didn't know I was gonna move, I thought we'd have more time."

Faolán pulled at the tear in the knee of his slacks, threads of blood-stained wool unraveling beneath his fingers.

"I understand why you stopped me," Faolán said. "Why you didn't trust me not to run, 'cause that's exactly what I ended up doing. I touched you because I'd missed you, and you were so close to me again, and Billie Holiday was singing. But, I also did it because I've wanted to kiss you for a very long time, and maybe I fooled myself into thinking I had a chance."

The sting of his confession left no part of him untouched. Faolán kept his head down, not knowing what Luca would do, now that he'd bared his soul. And as he ran through the reasons why Luca would leave, Luca rose from his chair and closed the gap between them.

Faolán pressed his hands against the table, steadying himself as Luca moved closer, the rickety shelves at his back giving him no room to move. He closed his eyes as Luca's lips brushed against his own, soft and tentative.

"Look at me."

Faolán opened his eyes and held Luca's stare, not sure if he was dreaming now, still asleep in the back of the taxi, traveling down quiet streets, heading towards home.

"I'm gonna tell you something, so just listen."

Faolán nodded.

"I know you don't know this, but years before Frankie and that god damn alley, you were the first guy I ever had eyes for. You were smart, and serious, and you made me believe there was magic right here in the city with all those stories you told me. You talked to me about important things, and you really wanted to know what I thought about everything, and not a lot of other people did. I thought you were pretty handsome too, and I hoped maybe you wouldn't mind if I kissed you. Maybe you'd be okay with that. But I never got up the nerve and then you started looking at girls, and I figured just being your pal was good enough.

"Luca, I-"

"No, listen. That letter I sent you, the one you never got. A lot of what I'm saying now, I wrote in that letter. I knew it might've been a mistake, but I wanted you to know. Then if you decided to come meet me after all, I'd know you felt the same way. So, what I'm saying is yeah, I've wanted to kiss you for a very long time as well."

Faolán waited for about thirty seconds after Luca fell silent, and when he was pretty certain the story had finished, he grabbed Luca by his shirt and pulled him close. Luca surged with him, pushing him back against the shelves and Faolán gasped as his aching shoulder struck the wood behind him, the impact taking his breath away. Luca pulled back.

"You alright?"

"No. Yeah, sorry. Keep going."

Faolán leaned into Luca's retreat, shifting forward, balancing precariously on the edge of the table as he pulled Luca back to him, and when their mouths finally met, the pain in his shoulder was forgotten.

He pushed his hands beneath Luca's shirt, dragged his fingers up the muscles of Luca's back, as he kissed him hungrily. And as Luca turned his attention to other parts of Faolán's body, and kissed a path down the tender line of his neck, Faolán whispered Luca's name and dug his fingers in to pull him closer.

Luca flinched hard. Faolán let him go.

"Did I hurt you?" Faolán asked, distracted by Luca's mouth, and the way his lips seemed almost darker after being so roughly kissed.

"No, right where you grabbed me, I think I got kicked there."

Faolán scooted back until he was steady and balanced again, careful of his proximity to the sharp angles at his back.

"Luca, maybe we-"

He let the rest of the suggestion go, that maybe they should move someplace less precarious, as Luca kissed him quiet. Luca moved slower this time, and Faolán took him by the belt and tugged him closer, figuring leather would be safer to grip than skin. Luca hummed against Faolán's mouth and laughed.

"Not letting go, huh?"

"Never."

Luca pushed Faolán's knees apart, leaning in for another kiss, and Faolán recoiled back against the shelves, sending books to the floor. He grabbed Luca's wrist.

"Christ, not that knee!"

"Ah... sorry." Luca put his hands up and backed away slowly. He dropped back down onto the chair, eyes closed, wearing his weariness like a second skin. He prodded at the bandage covering his stitches.

"Our bodies are like minefields..." Faolán dropped his head back against the shelves. A faded water stain had formed on the ceiling, where the corners met. He'd never noticed it before.

"You giving up on me already?"

"I'm not giving up," Faolán said quietly, "just getting a second wind."

"Okay. When you're done, wake me up. I think I know how to fix this problem."

"Will do."

Faolán lingered in the moments before they tried again. In some ways, this was like so many other times they'd spent together growing up, existing comfortably in each other's silence. But now, in the most fundamental of ways, things would never be the same, because the world had shifted that night and Luca loved him back. It was like he'd discovered a new color and now he could see it everywhere he looked, or maybe only he and Luca could see it, painted across each other's skin.

"So, you really think I'm handsome?" Faolán asked.

Luca grinned like he always did when Faolán spun up another story or tried to make him laugh. But the fondness in Luca's eyes, in the way that he looked at him now, made Faolán feel like the luckiest guy in the world.

"Yeah, this might go to your head, but when I saw you sitting by the fountain, you stopped me in my tracks. I even got a little nervous. I was kinda glad you were staring at your shoes so much tonight, so you didn't notice that I couldn't keep my eyes off you."

"Reiza said as much, you know."

"Did she? Guess I wasn't as subtle as I thought…"

With most of his body in varying states of pain, Faolán's short descent to the floor was less than graceful. He cursed quietly as he tried to land on his good leg, favoring his bad knee, overcompensating to protect his ribs, and pulling everything awkwardly on the way down. He hauled Luca up from the chair.

"What's this plan of yours? We take turns or something?"

"Well… Yeah."

"Oh, okay… So-" Faolán stepped back, not sure if he was supposed to wait or take the initiative.

"I'll go first," Luca said. He set his hands on Faolán's shoulders and backed him up against the table.

"What am I supposed to do?"

"I'm giving you the easy job. Keep your hands at your sides and stay where you are. Think you can do that?"

Faolán wavered for a moment before he lowered his hands.

"Yeah, but how will I know when it's my-"

Faolán lost the thread of his question as Luca kissed him again. Luca took his time now that he was in charge, slowing down when Faolán wanted to go faster, and each time he pulled back Faolán fought the urge to follow. He reached back and gripped the table, trying to anchor onto something, but when Luca stopped and looked at him like he was the only thing in the world, Faolán abandoned all attempts to stay still and grabbed Luca by the collar. Waiting for his turn went out the window and his kiss landed hard against the corner of Luca's mouth before he shifted and got it right.

He tried to go slower, careful not to re-open wounds, trying to avoid bruises, which was next to impossible in the shape they were in. If he had his way, if they weren't both on the edge of broken, he would be the one pushing Luca against the table. Kissing him hard.

"Whoa, I think you jumped the line there pal." Luca laughed as he grabbed Faolán by the wrists and wrestled his hands back down to his sides.

"Come on... Can't it be my turn?"

"You need me to help you out?"

"No... What do you mean?"

"Do you? Need me to help you out?"

Faolán stopped, not knowing what Luca was asking him anymore. Saying yes, meant admitting he couldn't handle it on his own, though the evidence so far leaned towards Luca being right. But saying yes also would mean that they could get back to kissing, and that was all he wanted to do right now.

"Maybe?" Faolán said, his confession stinging his pride.

"Alright, then go get my tie."

Faolán hesitated at the command, still embarrassed that he'd admitted he couldn't keep his hands to himself, and quickly putting together what Luca's request might mean. He shoved his hands into his pockets and didn't move.

"It's on the clothesline, I forgot to take it with me. You need me to show you where?"

"I can find it." Faolán raised his chin as a show of defiance, not sure why he wanted to push back, maybe just to show Luca they were still on even footing. He tamped it down and went to look.

Luca's tie hung between two of his undershirts, the silk still damp. Faolán unhooked the laundry line and dropped everything onto the loveseat, except what had been asked of him. He took his place once again between Luca and the table. Luca held out his hand.

"So, what. You're the boss now?" Faolán challenged again, wanting to see what Luca would do.

"Yeah, you got a problem with that?"

Luca pressed forward, matching Faolán's bravado with his own. The sudden advance sent Faolán back, off-balance but Luca caught him and steadied him just as fast.

"You got a problem with that?" Luca asked again, softer this time. He brushed the hair back that had fallen into Faolán's eyes.

Faolán shook his head.

Luca tucked the tie into his back pocket. Without a word, he unhooked the top button of Faolán's shirt, then set his finger on the second and waited, the pressure steady against Faolán's sternum.

Faolán reached up to where Luca stopped and started to take apart the buttons himself until Luca took him by the wrists and put an end to his progress. He didn't mind the correction this time as Luca kissed him while he guided his hands back down again.

"I don't know what I'm supposed to do," Faolán said.

"It's okay. Just let me."

Luca made slow work of undressing him, easing his suspenders from his shoulders and taking his time with all of the buttons as Faolán tracked his progress, and worked very hard at keeping his hands still. He raised his arms above his head tentatively, as Luca stripped him of his undershirt, unsure how far he could reach with all of his aching muscles, but Luca was careful with him and draped Faolán's shirts over the back of the chair when he was done.

The night felt different, as if they had crossed into something more serious, now that he stood stripped to his waist in the middle of his room. He stopped himself from listing forward and resting against Luca's chest and wished he didn't feel so exposed beneath the light.

"Turn around. Hands on the table."

Faolán hesitated again, dug in for only a moment, because once he turned his back to him, Luca would know so much more about the years they'd spent apart.

"You sure you're okay with this?" Luca asked.

"Yeah, you just gotta help me out."

Luca took him firmly by the shoulders and turned him around, and guided his hands onto the table. Faolán pressed his palms against the wood, bracing for Luca's reaction to what he would see.

He lowered his head, and waited in the quiet, the wooden table cool beneath his hands. Luca stood silent at his back.

He shuddered as Luca's fingers brushed the nape of his neck, too lost in his head to be ready for the touch. All of his attention now drawn to a single point on his body, so present that it felt as if a current stretched between them. Luca's fingers made a slow descent as they followed his spine, never touching the ragged scar across his shoulder blade, from the jagged edges of a bottle his stepfather had smashed on a kitchen floor, or the long faded marks across the small of his back from when he was held against a radiator until he promised never to talk back. But although Luca slowed as he passed them, he made no mention of the scars as he traced down the path of Faolán's bones and his fingers came to rest at the base of his spine.

"We don't have to do this. If you don't..."

"You weren't supposed to say anything. Please don't say anything. Don't ruin this."

Luca gripped the back of Faolán's belt and pulled him closer.

"Alright. Then bring your hands behind your back."

Faolán was so ready for Luca to push back, he barely heard the command. He quickly crossed his wrists behind his back, not wanting Luca to take it as a sign he was unsure. Dizzy with expectation, he swallowed down all of the questions he wanted to ask. They could come later. Luca moved closer, his lips brushed against Faolán's ear.

"There's one rule. You only follow my lead until you don't want to anymore, then we stop. You got it?"

Faolán closed his eyes and leaned back, and Luca took him in his arms.

"Yeah, I got it."

4

Faolán counted the number of times Luca wrapped the tie around his wrists, each loop drawing them closer together and making it harder to move. He got lost somewhere after four, when Luca stopped to kiss his shoulder and the back of his neck, before starting up again. Faolán pulled at his bindings while Luca worked, and held still only after he was told to quit his damn squirming.

"Is this what you like to do? To your..." Faolán didn't know how to frame the rest of the question. Didn't want to imply they were something now. It had only just begun.

"Sometimes. Hold these for a second."

Faolán gripped the ends of the tie as Luca adjusted the loops, shifting the damp silk until it laid flat against his skin. Luca took the ends back when he was done and knotted them together.

"Has anyone ever done this to you?" Faolán asked.

"Yep."

Faolán grew quiet, his mind filling up with thoughts of Luca kneeling before him with his head bowed and hands bound behind his back. Defiant, until Faolán took him by the chin and bent down to kiss him.

"You still there?" Luca asked. "See if you can get loose."

Faolán shook himself out of his thoughts. He closed his hands into fists.

"So, what? Like I mean it?"

"Yeah, like you mean it. Don't hurt yourself now. And keep it down."

Faolán shifted his stance wider for balance and yanked hard against the tie. When that got him nowhere, he tried again, slower this time, his slender wrists giving him about an inch of slack to work with. He could get free, eventually, if he worked smart enough. Faster, if he wasn't distracted by Luca at his back.

Luca knelt down and went to work again, wrapping up the space between Faolán's wrists and taking away his room to move. Faolán stopped struggling when Luca tightened the last knot, any chance of getting free now gone. He bowed his head, stretching out the space between his shoulder blades until they ached.

"It's not too tight? Make sure you can still move your wrists." Luca stayed at Faolán's back and slipped his finger beneath the folds, where the silk met skin.

Faolán tried once more, the dampness made it harder to move, but Luca hadn't been cruel, and the tie did no more than keep him in place.

He leaned back against Luca's chest, still trying to follow the strange thread that had started in Washington Square and ended here, with him tangled up in Luca's embrace. He didn't mind, in this moment, being under Luca's thumb, he'd pushed so hard against it growing up, that it surprised him a little that he was starting to like it.

Luca let go and stepped back, and Faolán stopped himself from moving with him, not wanting to sever the connection. But his floating only lasted a few moments before Luca grounded him again. He closed his eyes as Luca's hands settled onto his shoulders then traveled down, glancing over bruises in search of untouched skin, down biceps and forearms, across bound wrists and fingertips, until Luca's hands settled onto his belt and hauled him back.

Faolán gasped, caught off-guard as Luca pulled him into a rough embrace. He bit his lip, trying hard to keep quiet as Luca's hand slid down the front of his slacks, and stroked him roughly through the thin wool.

He dropped his head back, his legs growing unsteady as Luca got him hard, his briefs rubbing up the length of his cock beneath Luca's steady hand, the friction shifting between wonderful and maddening as the pleasure continued to build and he lost focus on everything but Luca's hand on him. Faolán rocked his hips forward, to show that he was ready, that he wanted more, that he was getting close.

Luca slowed and pulled his hand away. Faolán shook his head, shaky and breathless.

"Luca, you can't... just stop. Don't tease me like that."

"I'll tease you however I want," Luca growled, hot against his ear. He tightened his grip and pinned Faolán's arms against his sides.

The heat rose quickly up the back of Faolán's neck and the flush across his pale skin gave him away. He looked down at the floor, struggling with Luca's words, too worked up to respond, and embarrassed that the hard edge of the threat twisted him up inside and turned him on.

Luca turned Faolán around and backed him up against the table. The sly smile on his face said he knew exactly what his words had done. Luca took him by the chin.

"You still keen for this?"

Faolán nodded, trying not to show how flustered he felt. He wasn't used to this Luca at all, this beautiful man who wound him up, and got his heart racing, and stared at him like he was someone to be desired.

"I'm pretty sure this is the second time I've made you blush tonight." Luca crouched down and untied Faolán's shoes.

"When was the first?"

"When I loaned you that tie. I thought maybe you were embarrassed 'cause I was straightening you up in front of everybody, but I guess I was getting you all hot and bothered."

Faolán steadied himself against the table as Luca took his brogues, and then his belt, and then his slacks, pushing them down until they tangled around his ankles.

"Christ, how'd we miss that?" Luca asked.

Faolán followed Luca's gaze down past his obvious arousal to his battered knees. Dried blood painted his right shin crimson, and was still gummy across his knee where the rip in his slacks had been.

"It's fine, really. Let's handle it later."

"No, I'm not gonna leave you like this."

"Oh, come on" Faolán whispered as Luca sat him on the table and set off on his task.

Although he really wanted to get back to being groped, his knees did need patching up and cleaning. Faolán kicked until he worked his slacks from around his ankles and onto the floor. His socks took longer to shed, but he managed after some work, and added them to the pile.

Of all the ways he'd imagined his first time with Luca—and he'd imagined many—sitting tied up on his table in his underwear, while Luca rifled through his first-aid kit had never been one of them.

If he had his way, there would be far less light in the room, and he wouldn't ache so much, or be so tired, or so damn hard with no way to get off. He wouldn't care that he'd never grown as tall and strong as Luca, or that his shoulders weren't as broad and his arms not as muscled, now that Luca's gaze lingered on his body.

The first spark of an itch started at his temple, pulling at his attention as he was helpless to make it stop. He distracted himself as he waited by trying to will it away, but his effort only made him notice another nagging spot at the back of his head. Luca returned with a pile of first-aid supplies.

"Okay, let's see if we need to operate."

"Before that, can you help me out?"

"With what?"

Faolán lowered his head, uncertain what Luca would do with his request, not being his turn yet. "My head itches."

Luca set his supplies down and obliged without comment. He went in with both hands, raking his nails against Faolán's temples, then back and forth through his hair, grazing across his scalp and down to the nape of his neck. A soft moan escaped Faolán's lips as Luca dug his fingers in harder, his scalp tingling, and his thoughts growing fuzzy.

"Look at you. Hasn't anyone touched you like this?" Luca combed his fingers through Faolán's hair, taking his time sweeping it back into place. He took Faolán by the chin, his grip gentle and steadying. "You really are something..."

Faolán smiled, drowsy and contented, and practiced keeping still and waiting his turn. He floated as Luca straightened him up, letting the hand anchor him as he drifted, and reluctantly came back down only when Luca stepped back and let him go. Luca winked at him when he opened his eyes, then pulled up a chair and got back to work.

"Was that you asking me if I've been with anyone?"

"I don't know what you got up to in Boston. You kinda kissed me like you might have."

Faolán followed Luca's hands as he cleaned away the blood from his shin, only noticing now that Luca still favored his right hand, the knuckles stiff beneath the bandages.

"No," Faolán said. "I just kissed you like I've always wanted to."

Luca stopped and stared up at him thoughtfully, then went back to patching him up. He slowed when he started on Faolán's knee, careful with his work, inspecting the damage which despite the blood, he announced, wasn't too bad and that Faolán would live to fight another day, though he might have to give his getaway sticks a rest tomorrow.

Faolán tried not to smile and encourage anymore corny jokes, as Luca picked out pieces of grit and glass from his skin, and burned his wounds with iodine.

"Your wrists still okay?"

Faolán pulled against the tie as Luca secured a bandage across his knee. He'd gotten used to being bound as the night stretched on, countering against the way his weight shifted back on his heels when he stood, aware that everything seemed further away since he couldn't reach out when he wanted. But he'd stopped thinking of his restraints as anything more than an effective yet frustrating way to get him to stick to the rules of Luca's game.

Luca dragged his chair closer and pushed Faolán's knees apart, anchoring his hands on the places that weren't damaged. Faolán braced against the table and leaned back as Luca kissed a path up the inside of his thigh, and inhaled sharply when Luca's tongue flicked across tender skin.

"You need me to untie you?"

"Are you done with me?"

Luca hooked his fingers in the waistband of Faolán's briefs and tugged them low on his hips.

"Does it look like I'm done with you?"

"God, I hope not... Can we... I gotta perfectly good bed right over there."

Luca sat back and squinted at the far corner, where with some work and straightening, doubled as a bedroom. He pushed Faolán's knees back together and patted them gently.

"You stay here."

Faolán did as he was told, reeling from the sudden stop and start of everything, wondering if he should've kept quiet and let Luca keep going.

Luca stood before the Murphy bed, the metal frame locked against the wall and out of the way. He latched his fingers into the frame and pulled hard. The bed made a loud creaking noise but didn't move.

"I thought you said it was perfectly good." Luca grabbed the top of the frame and braced himself.

"Luca-"

"I know what I'm doing."

"Wait! I rigged an extra hook on the side so it won't come down on my head. Left side, towards the top. Please, don't break it. I can't afford another one."

Luca found the second hook and slowly lowered the bed to the floor.

"Why do you have... four blankets on your bed? It's August."

"I get cold in the morning, and I like the weight."

"But now you've got me."

Luca hauled Faolán off the table, sweeping him up in his arms like a bride at the threshold.

"What are you doing?"

"Taking you to bed."

"It's five steps, at most. I can still walk."

"Well, I wanted to throw you over my shoulder like Tarzan, but I didn't think your ribs or my body could handle any more damage."

Faolán struggled, but with his wrists tied, and trapped in Luca's arms his battle quickly became futile.

"I don't think you want me to drop you." Luca adjusted his grip and waited. "I'm really enjoying your damsel routine, but if you keep at it, were both gonna end up on the floor."

Faolán slumped against Luca's chest, defeated.

"Are you finished?" Luca asked.

"I think so."

Luca took the five steps back to the bed and sat Faolán down on the edge, the metal frame creaking under his weight. Faolán had never given a thought about how narrow his bed was, but now he wondered how they were both going to fit on it when they were done.

He took the initiative and tried to move to the center of his bed, but moving backwards with his hands bound was harder than he thought. He collapsed back, trapping his arms at an awkward angle beneath his body and a jolt of pain shot through his shoulder sharp enough to make him lightheaded. He barely registered Luca hauling him up and pulling the tie from around his wrists, until he caught his breath and the pain began to subside. Luca knelt before him, searching for what was wrong.

"Are you alright? Jesus, you scared me."

Faolán gripped his shoulder, the throbbing starting to fade now that he was upright.

"My shoulder's kinda worse off than it looks, but I'm okay, I swear. I just got it stuck at a bad angle..."

Luca sat beside him on the bed and rested his hand gently on his knee. Faolán knew what was coming next.

"Maybe we should call it a night. We're both pretty banged up, and I don't wanna hurt you any more than you already are... It's almost, what? Four in the morning?"

"Call it a night?" Faolán swayed as he stood, unsteady on his feet. Luca reached out to stable him. Faolán pushed his hand away. "Are you kidding me? I just got you back. It's my goddamn birthday. We're doing this, savvy?"

Faolán ignored Luca's uncertainty and crawled to the center of his bed, smoothing out the rumpled sheets and blankets along the way. He moved slowly, mindful of his shoulder and knees, and tried not to appear too off-balance now that he was taking the lead.

He laid down on his back and tucked his pillow beneath his head, sinking deep into the thin mattress, where the springs had gone loose from wear. He raised his arms, careful with the left, unsure if he had the range of motion until they came to rest above his head. He crossed his wrists and stared up at the ceiling as his body settled, and the pull of being still slowed him down.

"This way works." Faolán raised his head to see if Luca was still watching. "You can tie my wrists together like this. Then just tie the end to the springs below the mattress."

"Fae..."

"I can do this. Can we still do this?"

"Your shoulder— "

"—doesn't hurt like this. I swear. Do you still want to?"

"Of course I do. Look at you."

"Then tie me to the bed already. Before I pass out."

Luca relented after some hesitation, and bound Faolán's wrists again, more careful this time and not as tight. Faolán yanked his wrists free from the loops and fought back until Luca pinned him down and trussed him properly.

"You really are something, you know that?"

"Something? I thought I was smart, serious..."

"Don't forget handsome." Luca snapped the waistband of Faolán's briefs.

Faolán dug his heels into the bed and raised his hips to let Luca take the last of his clothes. He grew self-conscious again, lying stretched out and bare before someone who mattered so much. He shifted atop the rough blankets, and pulled against the tie to keep the rest of his body still.

"It looks like I've been holding you hostage in here, treating you badly." Luca stood at the foot of the bed and rolled up his sleeves, still fully dressed at the end of this long night. "If the cops busted in, they'd arrest me for kidnapping."

"If the cops busted in, they'd arrest us for much more than that, and you know it," Faolán said. "Now turn off the lights."

Luca watched him for a few moments longer, then did as he was asked and cast the space into darkness. He opened the curtains by the bed and stood silhouetted in the window.

On the surface, Faolán could see how all of this might seem sinister, being tied down and watched from the shadows, beaten up and aching. But unlike Luca's dark scenario, his heart had finally slowed once the lights turned off, and he was exactly where he wanted to be.

Luca returned to the foot of the bed and unbuckled his belt. Faolán raised his head from the pillow as the weight of the leather settled against his ankles, but allowed Luca to bind him without a fight. Luca looped the belt around the frame at the foot of the bed and locked him in place.

"Now fight it. Yes, like you mean it, and no, don't hurt yourself. See if you can get out."

"You know I can't, not like this."

"Try. For me."

With only one good shoulder he didn't have a chance, he couldn't brace against anything, he could barely twist his hips, but he dug in and fought like he meant it, like he had something to lose, because Luca had asked. Faolán strained against his bonds until his entire body ached and left him gasping. He fought until Luca's hand settled over his heart and pushed him gently back against the bed.

"You want me to try again?"

Luca sat down beside him. He shook his head.

"No, you did good."

Faolán closed his eyes, still breathing hard, as Luca traced his fingers down the length of his body, following the lines of his ribs, and across his stomach, the caress so light Faolán strained to press into it, and arch his back to give it weight, but bound so tightly he could do neither. As the night went on, he was quickly learning how Luca liked things, that he tended to linger, and to watch, that he liked to take his time, that he would take him apart slowly.

He tried not to give himself away as Luca mapped out the landscape of his body and discovered all of the places that made him gasp, and writhe, and shudder, while avoiding the one place he needed to be touched the most.

A shudder pushed through his body as Luca's mouth brushed across his hipbone, followed by the warm flick of his tongue, and a sharp scrape of teeth against skin. Faolán dropped his head back against the pillow, his breath shaky as Luca teased the oversensitive tip of his cock, first with his fingers and then with his tongue. He closed his hands into fists as Luca took him in his mouth, pulled back to the tip, then engulfed him again.

He lost count of how many times he begged Luca not to stop, or tried and failed to hold still. He was so close now, brain sparking and overwhelmed, his orgasm building as Luca brought him to the edge. Then Luca stopped and pulled back, leaving him desperate.

Luca's hand slid over his mouth and pinned him against the pillow. Faolán inhaled hard and fast through his nose, his protests stifled against Luca's warm fingers.

"Weren't you the one saying we gotta keep it down?" Luca leaned in close and whispered in Faolán's ear. "No matter how much I like it, you gotta stop calling my name, or you're gonna get us both in hot water. Can you do that?"

Luca pulled his hand away. Faolán shook his head, too worked up to be anything but honest.

"You need me to help you out?" Luca asked.

"Please."

Faolán's moans pushed against Luca's unrelenting hand as he was silenced once more. He struggled in vain to shift his hips forward, as Luca stroked him slower this time, and the waves of pleasure pushed through his body. He pressed his hands against the wall above his head and dug his heels against the mattress, unable to hold on anymore as Luca took him over the edge, shuddering as his climax radiated out through his limbs and left him floating.

He stayed quiet when Luca gave him his voice back, still heady and drifting while Luca pulled apart the knots around his wrists and the belt from his ankles. He didn't move even after he was free to, his wrists still crossed above his head, as Luca found a towel and cleaned him, yielding when Luca bent down to kiss him.

"I'm putting this on my list of ways I want to see you again," Luca said.

"You've got a list?"

"Started it right now," Luca tapped his temple. "Keeping it all in here."

Luca sat down heavily on the edge of the bed and began to un-button his shirt, his movements slow, his eyes half-closed. Faolán reached out and stilled Luca's hand.

"Let me do that."

Faolán dragged himself out of bed and stood naked before Luca in the dark, whatever self-consciousness he'd felt was now long forgotten. Luca leaned forward until his head came to rest against Faolán's chest and he let out a long sigh that warmed Faolán's skin. Faolán ran his fingers gently through Luca's hair.

"Luca?"

"I'm awake."

Luca flicked his tongue against Faolán's chest and groaned as he was hauled to his feet and wrestled out of his clothes. Faolán steadied him when he swayed.

Now that he'd reached skin, Faolán ran his hands along the planes of Luca's broad shoulders, fingers traveling down the tight muscles of Luca's arms, and across the bruises that darkened his abdomen. He still couldn't quite believe that he could touch Luca like this, after wanting to for so long, and now here Luca was standing naked before him, cock flushed and hard, aroused because of him. And because he could, he pulled Luca close and kissed him open-mouthed and slow.

"You know, I think it's finally my turn," Faolán said when he was finished with Luca's mouth.

"Is that right?"

Luca fell back onto the bed and pulled Faolán down with him. They stayed like that, wrapped up in each other's arms, too tired to do much else until Faolán reached down and stroked his thumb across the head of Luca's cock.

"I haven't gotten you off yet. You still want me to, right?"

Luca laughed as he kissed him again. "Well, when you ask me all romantic like that..."

"Let me go, I gotta get something first."

"Do I have to?"

Faolán pulled himself from Luca's embrace, enjoying the switch of Luca being impatient now. He knelt down before his dresser and eased open the creaking bottom drawer, trying to keep as quiet as he could.

"What are you doing down there? I'm sure we can manage."

"Get comfortable, I'll be one second." Faolán stopped and turned back. "And both hands behind your head. I don't want you getting started without me."

"What, so you're the boss now?"

"Yeah, you gotta problem with that?"

Luca laced his fingers behind his head and laid back on the pillow. "No, sir."

A dozen scenarios pushed into Faolán's head sparked from Luca's two words of obedience. He tucked them away for later and got back to his task. He dug through the depths, past the shampoo and hair tonic and his shaving kit and piled his random finds on the floor beside him as he searched.

"What are you looking for?" Luca asked.

"Vaseline."

"Why do you keep it in there? Every time you get in the mood, you gotta get out of bed and go excavating."

"What? I dunno, this is my medicinal and hygiene drawer. It falls into that category."

"Okay. I'm not gonna argue with you. So, what are we about to do?" Luca asked.

"I was gonna give you a hand job... Found it." Faolán closed his hand around the small glass jar and sat back on his heels, only then realizing what Luca's question meant. "Oh... I hadn't thought... Did you want to? I suppose we could..."

"I wasn't asking. I think if we tried to fuck right now, we'd break each other."

Faolán turned the jar over. He nodded, not sure if Luca could see him in the dark.

"I'm keen for that hand job though, if you're still offering. Vaseline, huh? No one will ever accuse Faolán Donovan of not being a gentleman."

"Jesus. I just wanted to do it how I like it. You keep it up and I'm gonna swap this with the VapoRub."

"Alright," Luca laughed, "get back over here with your petroleum jelly. Show me how you like it."

Faolán left the clutter on the floor behind him and made his way back to the bed. Luca lay as he had left him, stretched out and aroused, hands still behind his head. The top sheet was bunched down around his ankles and whatever blankets had been on the bed now lay in a pile on the floor.

"So, this is your view?" Luca asked.

"I usually turn that way," Faolán pointed towards the windows, where the pale curtains rippled slowly and the first of the delivery trucks rumbled past below. He climbed over Luca and settled against his side. "But looking at you ain't too bad."

He drew slick lines across Luca's abdomen, his fingers shiny with Vaseline, watching as the muscles tightened beneath his touch. He closed his hand around Luca's cock and found his rhythm, adjusting his pace as Luca's breath slowed and deepened, drawn to the way Luca showed his need. Desire made him beautiful, the way he bit his lip to stay quiet and locked his hands into fists beneath his head, as he struggled to keep them in place. Faolán traced his thumb across the head, the slit already slick, and the motion coaxed a quiet and needful sound from Luca's lips. Luca turned away.

"No, look at me. You don't get to hide that face."

Luca turned back to him, his pupils dark and wide.

When Faolán jerked off it always ended up frenzied and fast, aching to release, but Luca was at his mercy now and he didn't want this moment to end, so he slowed his hand to draw it out. He pressed closer and kissed him, wanting to taste him, and breathe in the soft sounds Luca made. Faolán ran his hand up the underside of Luca's cock, stroked steady and slow across the head, knowing that he would be desperate and begging by now, if it was still Luca's turn.

And perhaps because he wasn't bound, or because he was too close to be patient anymore, Luca gave up staying still and reached down and forced Faolán's hand faster, his fingers slipping between Faolán's own.

"Oh, I see. So, your rules don't apply to you?"

Luca's quick nod and quiet moan against Faolán's mouth served as enough of an answer.

Faolán fell back into the kiss and let Luca take the lead, and set the pace to finish himself off. Luca gasped quietly as he came, spilling onto their fingers. Faolán pulled him close and continued their kiss as Luca stilled and his breathing slowed.

"I don't think it was ever my turn tonight."

Faolán searched the bed until he found the towel, discarded on the floor by the blankets. He took his time cleaning Luca, getting lost in it for a while until Luca wrestled the towel from his hands and tossed it across the room. Faolán untangled the sheets and draped them over their tired bodies. Luca pushed his side back down.

"You're impossible," Faolan said, "but I'm gonna keep you anyway."

"Is that you trying to sweet talk me now?"

"Is it working?"

On the other side of the wall, came the familiar creak of metal springs and the soft thump of his neighbor's bed being closed up for the day. Luca kissed the bruise at the corner of Faolán's mouth.

Faolán rolled onto his back and reached his arm up toward the ceiling. Fading red lines marked his wrist, from when he'd struggled too hard, but he didn't care if they left bruises, he was already covered with so many, and these he didn't mind. Luca reached up and traced the lines across Faolán's wrist.

"You're starting to get that melancholy look," Luca said. "What's going on in that head of yours?"

Faolán shook his head and strained to reach higher. Luca took him by the wrist and guided his arm back down.

"Not melancholy, just thinking..."

"No regrets though, right?"

"God, no. You're stuck with me now... If you want me. I dunno, I just wish it all hadn't taken so long."

Faolán pulled the pillow from beneath Luca's head and tucked it under his own. He curled up on his side, to face the window and watch the colors change as the morning came, but for the first time with the weight of Luca settled warm and heavy against his back, holding him close.

"Promise me. We don't look back, okay?" Luca said.

"Okay."

"And we make up for lost time," Luca whispered against the nape of his neck. "Become friends again, but with you know... twice the kissing."

Faolán closed his eyes, drifting off as the city around them woke up.

"I'll hold you to that."

ABOUT THE AUTHOR

Enola Wilder is a queer author who writes steamy M/M fiction about flawed men who just want to be loved. She lives in the wilds of the New England with her forty-five plants.

Join My Newsletter

Be the first to know about new releases, upcoming titles, and get a free bonus epilogue for ***Reunion: Bachelors in a Bind, Book 1***

https://subscribepage.io/enolawilder

Website: www.enolawilder.com

Tumblr: enolawilder.tumblr.com

www.ingramcontent.com/pod-product-compliance
Lightning Source LLC
Chambersburg PA
CBHW061551310726
48972CB00008B/2715